JOHN HENRY

STEEL-DRIVING MAN

by
C.J. Naden

illustrated by
Bert Dodson

Folk Tales of America

Troll Associates

PROLOGUE

This John Henry is a pretend person. But there might have been a real John Henry. Some say there was, and that he was born in Tennessee and that he died in 1870. They say there really was a race between a man and a machine, just like the story tells.

If there was a real John Henry, he probably wasn't eight feet tall. And he probably wasn't quite as strong as all the stories say.

But none of that really matters. What does matter is the spirit of John Henry, the spirit that says "I can do it, and I can do it well." John Henry is part of anyone who ever feels that way.

Library of Congress #79-66317
ISBN 0-89375-304-1/0-89375-303-3 (pb)

10 9 8 7 6 5 4 3

John Henry was a steel-driving man. The biggest, the best, the fastest, the strongest steel-driving man anywhere. Ever.

Folks knew right away that John Henry was something special. Right from the moment he was born. That was way down South in cotton country. There just had to be something special about a brand-new baby that weighed thirty-three pounds. And talked.

People think John Henry was born with a hammer in his hand. But he wasn't. He was probably three weeks old before he picked up his daddy's five-pound hammer and started to swing it.

And people think that right after he was born, John Henry said to his mama, "I'm a steel-driving man, and I'll die with a hammer in my hand." But he didn't. What he said was, "I'm hungry."

You can bet that John Henry's mama and daddy were pretty surprised to see such a big baby. And they were even more surprised that he could talk.

"As long as you're talking, John Henry," said his mama, "why don't you tell us what you want for your first meal?"

"I'll be glad to, Mama," said young John Henry, "and I thank you kindly for asking."

John Henry was very polite from the start. That was one of the reasons that people sort of took to him. The other reason was that he had a nice face. He had large, dark eyes and a smiley mouth.

"Mama and Daddy," said John Henry, "for my first meal, I would be mighty pleased to have seven ham bones, three pots of giant cabbages in gravy, a large pile of turnip greens, and a kettle or two of black-eyed peas."

"Why, John Henry," cried his mama, "you're only ten minutes old! You can't eat that much food."

"I beg to differ, Mama," said John Henry, "but I'm a natural boy on the way to being a natural man. Eating is just a natural thing for me."

Now John Henry's mama and daddy didn't even eat that much food in a month. And they certainly didn't have that much food in their little cabin.

So John Henry's daddy decided that he'd better go ask the neighbors for some. But he didn't get very far. The neighbors were all standing right outside the front door. News of the very special baby had traveled fast. The neighbors were carrying ham bones and giant

cabbages and turnip greens and black-eyed peas.

When all the food was spread out on the table, young John Henry got right up and walked over to it. He took one look, smiled, and sat down to eat, with a large napkin tied around his neck.

It didn't take long for everyone to see that eating was a natural thing for John Henry, just like he said.

After that, John Henry grew. When he was two weeks old, he couldn't sit on his daddy's knee anymore. He was too heavy, and his feet touched the floor.

By the time he was four weeks old, he was swinging his daddy's hammer against rocks and stones outside the cabin. And *that's* when he said to his mama, "I'm a steel-driving man, and I'll die with a hammer in my hand."

John Henry's mama wasn't one bit happy to hear that kind of talk. So one day she took the hammer away. "I don't want you to be a steel-driving man," she said to John Henry, "and that's that. You'd better try something else."

John Henry tried lots of things. And he was good at everything he tried. But nothing felt just right. Nothing felt as good as that hammer in his hand.

Pretty soon John Henry had grown into a man. And he was big. Some say he was eight feet tall. Maybe so, maybe not. But he certainly was big.

Now that he was grown, John Henry knew it was time to do something serious with his life. Maybe I'll go to the fields and pick cotton, he thought. So one morning he marched on down to the cotton fields.

John Henry walked up to the overseer on the cotton plantation, and told him that he'd like to pick cotton.

The overseer looked at John Henry and frowned. "You're sure the biggest fellow I've ever seen," he said, "but do you know anything about picking cotton?"

14

"No, sir," said John Henry, "but I'm a natural man. Picking cotton is just a natural thing for me."

The overseer couldn't think of anything to say to that, and it was pretty clear that he thought John Henry was a bragging fool. But then he had an idea.

"My very best picker can pick one bale of clean cotton every day," he said. "Suppose we agree that you match that record, and I'll hire you."

"I beg to differ, Mr. Overseer," said John Henry. "I won't match that record—I'll beat it. I'll hang a cotton sack from each shoulder and tie another one around my waist. And I'll pick you three bales of clean cotton every day."

Well, now the overseer knew for sure that John Henry was a bragging fool. But he thought he'd just take him down a peg or two, so he agreed to let John Henry try.

Everyone on the plantation gathered around to watch John Henry try to pick three bales of cotton in one day. They were all laughing and smiling and smacking each other on the back because they knew it wasn't possible to pick that much cotton in one day. Every cotton picker knew that. Everybody but John Henry.

John Henry put one cotton sack over his left shoulder and one cotton sack over his right shoulder. Then he tied one cotton sack around his waist. Off he went into the fields.

As John Henry started to work, he started to sing. He sang songs about the boll weevil and about cotton pickers and about life down on the levee in New Orleans.

It didn't take very long for everybody to see that picking cotton was a natural thing for John Henry. Just like he said.

That day John Henry picked three bales of clean cotton. Exactly. And the overseer hired him on the spot.

John Henry became the best cotton picker in the whole South. But he wasn't happy. The cotton in his hand just didn't feel right. Not like that hammer. So he thought that maybe he'd look around for some other work to do. But just about that time, something unusual happened.

John Henry was in town one day on an errand for the overseer when it happened. Now John Henry was the biggest and the strongest man around anywhere. But all of a sudden, something made him feel weak. It happened when he was walking along the street and ran smack into Polly Ann.

John Henry couldn't believe his eyes. Polly Ann was about the prettiest girl he'd ever seen. She had great big, dark eyes and a yellow ribbon in her hair. And John Henry just went weak all over.

Polly Ann kind of took a liking to John Henry, too. Pretty soon they started seeing each other every Saturday night, and then on Sundays.

In the fall, Polly Ann and John Henry were married. And John Henry figured that, except for the sad feeling about the hammer every once in a while, he was the happiest man anywhere.

Now cotton pickers don't make a lot of money. So John Henry and Polly Ann decided to set out to make their fortune someplace else.

Before they left, John Henry said goodbye to his mama and daddy.

"I'm sad to see you go, son," said his mama, "but you're a grown man now and married, too. You've got to make your own life, whatever it is." And John Henry's mama was sad because she knew that somewhere, someday, there was a hammer waiting for John Henry.

John Henry knew it, too. But he just smiled and kissed his mama and daddy goodbye.

Polly Ann and John Henry traveled around the country looking for just the right place to settle down and just the right job for John Henry. He tried lots of things. For a while he picked tobacco, and, sure enough, he turned out to be a natural tobacco picker. For a while he loaded crates and barrels and bales onto ships. And he turned out to be a natural dock worker. And for a while he drove a team of mules for a big company. And he turned out to be a natural mule driver.

But every once in a while, John Henry would get that sad feeling again. Because nothing, not tobacco or barrels or mules, felt right in his hands. Not like that hammer.

Then one day, John Henry and Polly Ann were walking through the hills of West Virginia. They were thinking that they liked the looks of the country, that maybe this was a good place to settle down.

21

And then, from over the next mountain, they heard a sound. And to John Henry it was the most beautiful sound in the world. It was the sound of hammers ringing out loud over the hills. It was the sound of hammers hitting steel.

John Henry said to Polly Ann, "I've found it. I've found what I've got to do."

Polly Ann remembered what John Henry's mama had said, and she looked a little sad. But she knew, sure as John Henry knew, that this was what he was meant to do.

John Henry and Polly Ann walked over the mountain, and, sure enough, there were the

hammers ringing. Men were hammering and singing and building the Big Bend Tunnel for the Chesapeake and Ohio Railroad. It wasn't a real big railroad or a real big tunnel. But it was going to go right through the mountain. And to John Henry, it was beautiful.

To build this tunnel through the stone mountain, the men had to drive rods of steel into the rock with their hammers. Then they put explosives in the holes and blew the rock away. Driving steel was a hard job. One man held the steel rod. He was called a shaker. The other man stood back and whomped the steel with his ten-pound hammer.

John Henry walked right up to the boss. His name was Captain Tommy.

"Captain," said John Henry, "I am here to drive steel for you." He said it quiet but straight out, just like that.

Now John Henry was a very big man, bigger than the Captain had ever seen. "You're big, all right," said Captain Tommy, "but I bet you don't know anything about driving steel."

"I beg to differ, Captain," said John Henry, "I'm a natural man. Driving steel, more than anything else, is just a natural thing for me."

Captain Tommy thought right off that John Henry was a bragging fool. But it was time for the men to break for lunch anyway. So the Captain decided to let them have a few laughs watching John Henry try to drive steel.

"Hey, Will," he called to his best steel shaker. "Come on over here and hold the rods for this natural steel-driving man."

25

The steel men all took to laughing when they heard that.

Little Will came running over to hold the steel spikes. When he saw the size of John Henry, he blinked a couple of times.

"Pick up a hammer," said Captain Tommy to John Henry, "and let's see what kind of steel-driving, natural man you are." All the other steel-driving men laughed some more and pounded each other on the back when they heard that. They knew that it takes a long while to learn how to lift that heavy hammer and whomp that steel spike just right.

John Henry smiled and picked up the hammer. Then he put it down again. "It's too light," he said to Captain Tommy. "I can't drive steel with such a light hammer."

"I've really got a bragging fool on my hands," thought the Captain. But all he said was, "We've got a twenty-pound hammer here. You're such a natural man, maybe you can use that."

The other steel-driving men were really laughing and stomping now. This was the best fun they'd had in a long time. They knew that no one, no matter how big, could handle that twenty-pound hammer for long.

John Henry just smiled and picked up the hammer. Then he winked at Polly Ann to let her know how good things were. "This hammer feels better," he said. "Let's go, Will."

So Will held the spike, and John Henry swung the twenty-pound hammer. Whomp! Right smack on the steel spike. Right smack in the center. And the spike went halfway through the rock, clean as you please. Will couldn't believe his eyes, and neither could Captain Tommy. And the other steel-driving men stopped their laughing and stomping and back-smacking.

And every one of them could see that steel driving was a natural thing for John Henry. Just like he said.

John Henry drove steel with that twenty-pound hammer for the next hour without stopping. He almost wore out Little Will, and Little Will was the best shaker around. And pretty soon the Captain had to start pouring water on the spikes, because John Henry was hitting them so fast they were smoking.

Finally, the Captain called to John Henry, "Stop! I can see that you're not a bragging fool. You're just what you say you are, a natural steel-driving man. And you're hired."

John Henry was so happy that he picked up Polly Ann and spun her around. He didn't even feel tired after all that steel driving. Just a mite thirsty. That hammer had felt just right in his hand. At last.

So John Henry and Polly Ann moved into a little company house near the railroad camp. Polly Ann planted a garden and tended to things, and John Henry drove steel. But it is said that once in a while, when John Henry came down with a cold or something, Polly Ann would take his place. And it is said that Polly Ann drove steel like the best of them. Maybe not quite as fast or as sure as John Henry, but then, John Henry was the best and the surest and the fastest steel driver anywhere. Ever.

What with Polly Ann and the little house and his work, John Henry believed that he was the world's happiest man. But then one day he got even happier. That was because one day John Henry and Polly Ann became the proud parents of a baby boy.

"I can tell," said John Henry to Polly Ann, "that this child is smart and beautiful like his mama. But I can also tell from the way he holds on to my finger that he is going to be a natural steel-driving man."

Polly Ann looked a little sad at that. But she didn't say a word.

Every working day, John Henry drove steel, with Little Will holding the spikes. John Henry's mighty hammer flew, and he sang as he hammered, all about a natural steel-driving man who died with a hammer in his hand.

Sometimes Little Will, who everyone knew was the best shaker around, had to beg John Henry to stop driving steel for a while, just so he could take a rest. John Henry never seemed to get tired, but he always stopped for his friend Little Will.

From miles around, people would come just to watch John Henry at work on that Big Bend Tunnel. It was truly a glorious show. His hammer sounded like thunder from the sky as it swung in a great circle over his head. Whoosh it went, and whomp it went, as it struck the steel rod square in the middle and drove it into the rock. Whoosh, whomp. Whoosh, whomp. Never once did John Henry miss a stroke. The sparks flew and John Henry sang. And it was truly a fine sight to see.

Some days Polly Ann would bring the baby and visit John Henry in the camp. On those days his hammer thundered like never before, and his songs grew louder, and his heart was full.

Then one day a city man in fancy clothes came into the railroad camp. He was carrying a strange-looking piece of metal.

"Captain Tommy," said the city man, "I have here a wonderful machine. It's called a steam drill. It can outdrill any five men in half the time."

Captain Tommy just laughed and shook his head. "City Man," he said, "I've got someone right here who can outdrill any ten men in one-quarter the time. I sure don't need your steam drill."

"Oh, I know what you mean, all right," said the city man. "I've heard all about John Henry. He's a steel-driving man, there's no doubt. But he can't beat my drill. And I'd like to lay down a little money that says so."

"Well, I know he can," said Captain Tommy, "and that's the end of it. I'm not a betting man."

Now John Henry at that time just happened to be taking a rest for Little Will's sake, and so he overheard the city man's talk. "Captain," he said, "I beg to differ, but I think we just ought to take this city man's bet. A natural steel-driving man can beat any machine there ever was, and I want to prove it."

The city man thought for sure that John Henry was a bragging fool. And he thought for sure that here was a good chance to sell his drill. "I say my machine can beat any man," he said.

"It can't beat a natural steel-driving man," said John Henry. "Why, before I'd let that

machine beat me, I'd die with a hammer in my hand." He said it quiet but straight out.

And so the race was planned. John Henry would get one-hundred dollars if he beat the machine, and Captain Tommy would get the machine free. If the machine won, the Captain had to buy it. Those were the terms of the bet.

On the morning of the great race, people gathered from miles around to see the natural man against the steam machine. Polly Ann was there with the baby, looking kind of sad and just a little worried. But John Henry winked at

her and smiled. Captain Tommy was looking a little worried, too, and so was Little Will. But John Henry just kept smiling.

"No machine can beat a steel-driving man," he said. "And that's what I am."

The city man turned on his steam drill and John Henry picked up his great hammer. A judge blew the whistle, and the race began. Soon the air was filled with the hiss and clatter of the steam drill and the whoosh and the whomp of John Henry's mighty hammer swinging out and striking the steel. And just like always, he sang as he worked—songs about a natural steel-driving man.

Hour after hour the race went on. The machine was hissing and clattering and John Henry was hammering and singing.

"How are you doing?" Little Will kept asking John Henry.

"I'm doing just fine," John Henry told him between songs. "Just keep holding those spikes. No machine is ever going to beat this steel-driving man."

After about five hours, both the machine and John Henry stopped for a few minutes. The city man had to replace a worn part in the machine, and John Henry felt as though he could use a drink of water.

"Are you doing all right?" Little Will asked.

This time John Henry just nodded. Then he asked, "Who's winning?"

"I think it's about even," Little Will told him.

"No machine can even tie a natural steel-driving man," John Henry said. "And now I'm going to prove it for sure."

When the whistle blew for the race to continue, John Henry picked up two twenty-pound hammers, one in each hand. The machine whirred and clattered, and John Henry's mighty hammers whooshed and whomped. It was a sight to remember.

Hour after hour. Whirr and clatter. Whoosh and whomp. The whole mountain was filled with the noise of steel driving. But there was no more singing from John Henry. Just the steady whoosh and whomp of his two mighty hammers.

It seemed as if the drilling would never end. But then the last whistle blew. The race was over.

The judges ran over to the drilling holes. After a few minutes, they declared, "John Henry has drilled the deepest and the biggest holes. John Henry has beaten the machine!"

Everybody clapped their hands and stomped around and laughed and carried on, thinking how wonderful it was that John Henry had beaten the steam drill. Everybody except the city man. He just left the drill where it was and walked away.